★ **Sports Greats** ★

Top 10 Teams in Basketball

Jamal Tyson Hinnant

Enslow Publishing
101 W. 23rd Street
Suite 240
New York, NY 10011
USA
enslow.com

Published in 2017 by Enslow Publishing, LLC.
101 W. 23rd Street, Suite 240, New York, NY 10011

Copyright © 2017 by Enslow Publishing, LLC.

All rights reserved.

No part of this book may be reproduced by any means without the written permission of the publisher.

Library of Congress Cataloging-in-Publication Data

Names: Hinnant, Jamal.
Title: Top 10 teams in basketball / Jamal Tyson Hinnant.
Description: New York : Enslow Publishing, 2017. | Series: Sports Greats | Includes bibliographical references and index.
Identifiers: LCCN 2015050574| ISBN 9780766076037 (Library Bound) | ISBN 9780766075993 (Paperback) | ISBN 9780766076006 (6-pack)
Subjects: LCSH: Basketball—United States—History—Juvenile literature. | Basketball teams—United States—History—Juvenile literature.
Classification: LCC GV885.5 .H36 2017 | DDC 796.323/64—dc23
LC record available at http://lccn.loc.gov/2015050574

Printed in the United States of America

To Our Readers: We have done our best to make sure all website addresses in this book were active and appropriate when we went to press. However, the author and the publisher have no control over and assume no liability for the material available on those websites or on any websites they may link to. Any comments or suggestions can be sent by e-mail to customerservice@enslow.com.

Photos Credits: Cover, p. 1 Jason Miller/Getty Images Sport/Getty Images; throughout book, Andrew Rich/E+/Getty Images (basketball texture background); p. 5 Christian Petersen/Getty Images Sport/Getty Images; pp. 7, 8 Peter Read Miller/Sports Illustrated/Getty Images; pp. 11, 20, 27, 40 John W. McDonough/Sports Illustrated/Getty Images; p. 12 Mark Wilson/Getty Images News/Getty Images; p. 15 Rosato/Sports Illustrated/Getty Images; p. 16 Jim Davis/The Boston Globe via Getty Images; p. 19 Allsport/Allsport/Getty Images; p. 23 Manny Millan /Sports Illustrated/Getty Images; p. 24 V.J. Lovero/Sports Illustrated/Getty Images; p. 28 Andy Lyons/Getty Images Sport/Getty Images; p. 31 Vince Bucci/AFP/Getty Images; p. 32 Jeff Gross/Getty Images Sport/Getty Images; p. 35 Ronald Martinez/Getty Images Sport/Getty Images; p. 36 Ezra Shaw/Getty Images Sport/Getty Images; p. 39 Greg Nelson /Sports Illustrated/Getty Images; p. 43 PAUL BUCK/AFP/Getty Images; p. 44 JEFF HAYNES/AFP/Getty Images.

Contents

Introduction 4

1982-83 Philadelphia 76ers 6

2010-11 Dallas Mavericks 10

2007-08 Boston Celtics 14

1993-94 Houston Rockets 18

1988-89 Detroit Pistons 22

2013-14 San Antonio Spurs 26

2000-01 Los Angeles Lakers 30

2014-15 Golden State Warriors 34

2012-13 Miami Heat 38

1995-96 Chicago Bulls 42

   Glossary 46

   Further Reading 47

   Index 48

★ Introduction ★

If you are a basketball fan, you become a part of the game—booing when your favorite team is losing and cheering when a championship is won. Whether it's the 1960 Boston Celtics, 1980 Los Angeles Lakers, or 2015 Golden State Warriors, every championship team has traces of perfection.

The league was founded in New York City in 1946 as the Basketball Association of America (BAA). After battling to win fans, the BAA purchased its rival, the National Basketball League (NBL), and formed the National Basketball Association (NBA). The league adopted its new name on August 3, 1949.

Largely accepted as the world's most dominant men's professional basketball league, the NBA is made up of thirty teams that are split into two conferences: the Eastern Conference and the Western Conference. The conferences are made up of three divisions of five teams. Along with the opportunity to break records and win awards each year, teams also have three levels of possible victory. They can champion their division and then their conference. The conference winners face off for the most prized victory: the NBA Championship. The Boston Celtics and Los Angeles Lakers lead the league with the most NBA Championships won by franchises with seventeen and sixteen wins, respectively. To give you a better idea of how impressive that is, no other team in the league has more than six rings, and thirteen teams have never won at all.

Over time, the NBA introduced new regulations to improve how the game is played. The 24-second shot clock was introduced in the 1950s to speed up the pace of the game, which made them more fun to watch. People had interest in this league from the early days, but popularity soared high in the 1970s, when rookies like Kareem Abdul-Jabbar, Magic Johnson, Moses Malone, Julius Erving, and Larry Bird joined. Since then, basketball has been growing all across the world. Teams have put a lot of effort into searching for and developing the next big NBA superstar, which has increased the level of competition. The league also attracts a lot of international players.

It can be difficult to compare the best teams to each other because major changes have been made to the rules, the length of the season, and the number of competing teams since the late 1940s. All these factors affect how the game is played. While every championship team deserves to be on this list, we couldn't choose them all. The greatest teams did more than just dominate on the court; they influenced the world and forever changed the way basketball is played. Here are our picks for the top ten best teams in the history of the NBA!

Los Angeles Laker Pau Gasol leads his team in celebration after the Lakers defeated the Boston Celtics in Game 7 of the 2010 NBA Finals.

1982-83 Philadelphia 76ers

Starting Lineup: Maurice Cheeks, Andrew Toney, Julius Erving, Bobby Jones, Moses Malone

Season Record: 65–17

Coach: Billy Cunningham

The Philadelphia 76ers have built an NBA franchise legacy that has captured the hearts of fans worldwide. They were one of the first eleven teams to help grow the NBA into all that it is now. To date, nine players that have played for the Sixers are in the National Basketball Hall of Fame. This list will have an addition soon because the Hall of Fame recently announced that retired point guard Allen Iverson is eligible for the Class of 2016. There's something special at the core of this franchise because even when they are losing, they are fun to watch.

The most popular—and undoubtedly most successful—76ers team was the 1982–83 team. That season, Philadelphia added a new big man, Moses Malone, to the center of their starting lineup. Malone led the team by averaging 24.5 points and 15.3 total rebounds per game throughout the regular season. He had strong support from guards Andrew Toney and Maurice Cheeks. Toney

1982-83 Philadelphia 76ers

Julius Erving, more popularly known as Dr. J, blows past Magic Johnson (32) as he drives to the basket. Erving was the most popular player on the Philadelphia 76ers and led his team to the 1983 NBA Championship.

Top 10 Teams in Basketball

Moses Malone celebrates after Philadelphia won Game 4 of the NBA Finals against the Los Angeles Lakers.

averaged 19.7 points per game (PPG), while Cheeks led unselfishly by adding 12.5 points and 6.9 assists per game.

What made this team so special was their most popular player, Julius Erving. Erving played a brand new style of basketball in the 1980s and forever changed the game. *Sports Illustrated* named Irving, better known as Dr. J, one of the forty most important athletes of all time. He led the team to three NBA Championships and was most known for his spectacular slam dunks. During this legendary season, Dr. J was a spectacular athlete to watch—an aggressive player with the right amount of finesse. Dr. J was all over the court and put up an average of 21.4 points and 3.7 assists per game on offense. On the defensive end, he had 1.6 steals with 6.8 total rebounds per game, the second highest rebounding average on his team.

When the Sixers added Moses Malone to their roster, they became an unstoppable force that almost swept the NBA Playoffs and only lost one of their postseason games. They were crowned 1983 NBA Champs.

The 76ers have an amazing legacy with players who were more than just great athletes—they were trendsetters! In the 1960s, Wilt Chamberlain's pure domination forced the NBA to make changes to the size of the court. Eleven-time All-Star Allen Iverson was one of the NBA's most legendary players. However, the best complete 76ers squad has to be the 1982–83 team. Dr. J introduced hang time by jumping and staying in the air for extended periods before passing or shooting. The team had a winning percentage of .793—the highest of the season. The 1982–83 76ers were one of the most talented teams in NBA history.

2010-11 Dallas Mavericks

Starting Lineup: Jason Kidd, Jason Terry, Shawn Marion, Dirk Nowitzki, Tyson Chandler

Season Record: 53-29

Coach: Rick Carlisle

When an unlikely team defies the odds and wins the championship, it creates the most inspirational team stories. The Mavericks' coaching staff was looking to add support to the great players they already had in Dirk Nowitzki and Jason Terry. They reached a trade agreement with the New Jersey Nets in 2008 for returning All-Star point guard Jason Kidd. Dallas had originally selected him as the second overall pick in the 1994 NBA Draft. After serving on several teams, he returned to Dallas with one goal in mind: help bring the team a championship. The Mavericks made it to the postseason in 2009 and again in 2010 but were eliminated early in the playoffs. In 2010, the Mavericks received the lift they needed when powerful seven-foot-one big man Tyson Chandler joined the team.

The Mavericks immediately noticed the impact of their new lineup, as they won 24 of the first 29 opening games. They finished

2010-11 DALLAS MAVERICKS

the regular season in second place in the Western Conference with a win-loss record of 57–25. If they would have had a completely healthy team, they might have topped the first-place Chicago Bulls, who had 62 season wins. A sprained knee benched the Mavs' leading scorer, Nowitzki, for nine games right in the middle of the season. Nowitzki averaged 23 points, 7 rebounds, and 2.6 assists per game. His absence was damaging; without Nowitzki, the Mavericks only won two of their next nine games. He returned to the court before the end of the season and managed to hold the Mavericks at the second best record in the NBA.

Another one of the Mavs' key offensive players, Caron Butler, also made the injured reserve list. During the first half of the season, Butler added 15 points and 4.1 rebounds per game. He suffered a ruptured right patellar tendon, though, that benched him for the rest of the season. Butler

Dirk Nowitzki takes it to the net during Game 5 against the Miami Heat. Returning after his injury, Nowitzki led Dallas to a championship season.

Top 10 Teams in Basketball

only played 29 games before he got hurt, which happened just four days after Nowitzki's injury.

The Mavericks relied heavily on small forward Shawn Marion to step up in Butler's absence. Marion completed the season posting 15 points, 4.1 total rebounds, and 1 steal per game to show that he was up for the challenge. This is an example of what made the 2010–11 Mavericks so special. Everyone was ready and willing to step in and fill the spaces needed to be the best team for every

President Barack Obama poses for a picture with the Dallas Mavericks during an event to honor the NBA Champions at the White House on January 9, 2012. President Obama congratulated the 2011 NBA Champions for claiming their first title by beating the Miami Heat 4–2 in the NBA Finals.

game. Jason Terry added to the speed, excelling during transitional plays and averaging 15.8 points and 4.1 assists per game. Chandler was excellent on defense with 10.1 points, 9.4 rebounds, and 1.1 blocks per game for the season.

The Mavericks continued to be a threat during the postseason because of players such as Shawn Marion and Jason Kidd, who performed well during clutch moments. The Mavs moved past Portland in a close six-game series. They didn't start to look like a championship team until the second round of the playoffs, as they dismantled the Los Angeles Lakers in a vicious four-game sweep. With the same energy, the Mavs outplayed fan favorites Kevin Durant, Russell Westbrook, James Harden, and the Oklahoma City Thunder in a 4–1 series upset. The Mavericks enjoyed a short celebration as they prepared for the greatest battle of the season. They were the underdogs in the NBA Finals against the super squad Miami Heat.

Although Nowitzki scored a game high of 27 points, Miami's LeBron James and Dwyane Wade collaborated to snatch Game 1 of the finals. Dallas regrouped in the final minutes of Game 2 and pulled one of the most memorable 15-point comebacks in NBA history. The Heat won Game 3 by 2 points. The Mavericks seemed to be playing better each night as they tied the series by winning Game 4. Nowitzki, Terry, Kidd, and Chandler helped close out the last three games to stop Miami in a 4–2 series. The 2010–11 Dallas Mavericks won the first NBA Championship in the team's history.

★ 2007-08 Boston Celtics ★

Starting Lineup: Rajon Rondo, Ray Allen, Paul Pierce, Kevin Garnett, Kendrick Perkins

Season Record: 67–15

Coach: Doc Rivers

Each year, franchises look to build their team by adding great defensive players to their roster. The Boston Celtics have used this as their recipe for success since the early years of their franchise with their first set of superstars.

In what still holds the title for the largest single-player trade in NBA history, the Celtics picked up Kevin Garnett in exchange for five of their players. When the Celtics first acquired Garnett, they had just finished the 2006–07 season with the second worst record in the league (24–58), which was also the second worst in their team's history. The 2006–07 season was unsuccessful because Boston was crippled by injuries.

Garnett was the puzzle piece that put the Celtics back together. With Paul Pierce healing from his foot injury and ten-time All-Star Ray Allen in the lineup, Garnett completed the new era Big Three, which mimicked the 1980s Celtics Big Three dynasty—Larry

2007-08 Boston Celtics

Bird, Robert Parish, and Kevin McHale. During this season, the Big Three were each averaging almost 20 points and 4 rebounds a game. Garnett didn't let a ball go to waste as he snatched 10.1 rebounds per game. Rookie point guard Rajon Rondo and big man Kendrick Perkins became household names, as well. Rondo immediately rose to All-Star status by netting 10.6 points, 5.1 assists, and 4.2 rebounds every game, while Perkins defended nicely with 6.9 points, 1.5 blocks, and 6.1 rebounds each game. The Celtics won more than 60 games during the regular season and sold out every home game. The Celtics had the best win-loss record in the league that season at 66–16.

The squad entered the 2008 NBA Playoffs as the number one seed. During the first round of the NBA Eastern Conference Playoffs, costly mistakes, such as not contending on defense, fouls, and missing easy baskets, dragged the Celtics and the Atlanta Hawks to seven games.

Kevin Garnett shoots a jumper against the Atlanta Hawks during the NBA Playoffs. Adding Garnett to the team seemed to be the missing piece to this team's puzzle.

Top 10 Teams in Basketball

The Big Three were determined to show why they were the best team in the league, and they completely took control of Game 7. The Celtics dominated the Hawks with a 34-point blowout of 99–65. The Cleveland Cavaliers tried to stop the Big Three by having fewer turnovers and more rebounds, but it wasn't enough. The Celtics narrowly outscored Cleveland to advance to the Eastern Conference Finals. It would take six games to defeat the Detroit Pistons to become the Eastern Conference Champions.

The Celtics faced off against Kobe Bryant and the Los Angeles Lakers in the finals. Head Coach Doc Rivers knew they could not take any chances against the Lakers. In order to win, they would

The Boston Celtics defeated the Los Angeles Lakers to win the NBA Finals 4 games to 2, and in the process they wrapped up the franchise's seventeenth NBA Championship. Captain Paul Pierce exults on the podium.

have to play as aggressively as they did during the regular season. These two teams were the most successful franchises in the NBA.

Boston established an early lead in the series by winning the first two games. Kobe Bryant dropped 36 points and carried the Lakers to victory in Game 3. That win shifted the momentum because the Lakers dominated the first quarter of Game 4, when they established the largest first-quarter lead in NBA Playoff history. The Celtics were determined not to let this game get away. With their backs against the wall, the Big Three found their groove again in the second quarter. They rallied from behind and outscored the Lakers in all of the next three quarters. They often double-teamed Kobe Bryant to limit his offensive effectiveness. Even the Celtics bench outscored the Lakers bench 35–15. Paul Pierce led the game with 20 points, which helped win Game 4. Los Angeles snatched Game 5, which brought the series to 3–2 with the Celtics ahead.

Game 6 was the ultimate showdown. Boston wanted to end the series but knew the Lakers would not go down without a fight. This game set the record for the most playoff games played in one season—twenty-six for the Celtics. The fatigue of a long postseason seemed to show in the first quarter because Boston missed many of their field goals. Somehow they gained a second wind, and the team started to emerge in the next three quarters to end Game 6 in a complete blowout. The final score was Celtics 131, Lakers 92. The Celtics were crowned the 2008 NBA Champions.

This was Boston's first NBA title since 1986. The team had a strong season of good chemistry, talent, and aggression on both ends of the court, which landed them on our countdown.

1993-94 Houston Rockets

Starting Lineup: Kenny Smith, Vernon Maxwell, Robert Horry, Otis Thorpe, Hakeem Olajuwon

Season Record: 53–29

Coach: Rudy Tomjanovich

When a team starts off the season as hot as the 1993–94 Houston Rockets did, every opponent tries their best to give that team its first loss of the season. The Rockets fought off the first fifteen teams to tie for the best opening record in the NBA. The last time a team had a start this strong dated back to the 1948–49 Washington Capitols. The record remained unbroken for another twenty-two years until the 2015–16 Golden State Warriors opened with twenty-four straight wins.

For the first fifteen games of the season, no team reached 100 points against the Rockets. The group was led by Hakeem Olajuwon, who was named NBA MVP and the Defensive Player of the Year for the season. Olajuwon was one of the league leaders in scoring, putting up 27.3 PPG, rebounding 11.9 shots per game, and blocking 3.71 shots per game. If you think the Rockets only had one hot player, think again. Their secret weapon on offense

1993-94 HOUSTON ROCKETS

Center Hakeem Olajuwon of the Houston Rockets goes up for two during a game against the Chicago Bulls.

Top 10 Teams in Basketball

rested in their unselfishness as a team. They moved the ball around through several teammates before scoring. Almost every player on the team had high per-game assist stats. Otis Thorpe posted 14 points and 10.6 rebounds to pick up where Olajuwon was out of reach. Vernon Maxwell added 13.6 points, 5.1 assists, and 1.7 steals per game. Robert Horry added 9.9 points and 5.4 rebounds, while Kenny Smith posted 11.6 points with 4.2 assists per game. Chris Jent came off their bench ready to play. He averaged 10.3 points followed by Mario Elie with 9.3 points. Their team shooting average was extremely accurate with most of their team shooting above 50 percent.

Their first season loss came from the Atlanta Hawks in a 133–112 blowout. The loss humbled the Rockets and reminded them that in order to be championship contenders, they couldn't take a single game for granted. Houston bounced back and went on another streak to win the next seven games for a 22–1 record. The Rockets finished the

Kenny Smith (right) and Vernon Maxwell (left) celebrate on the court. Maxwell came through with a big performance in Game 3 of the semifinals on the Rockets' road to the NBA Championship.

1993-94 Houston Rockets

regular season with a record of 53–29, which secured the top spot in the Midwest Division and second in the Western Conference.

Olajuwon led the team into the postseason, and they moved on to a challenging battle against the third-ranked Phoenix Suns. Houston started the first two games exactly the same—entering the last quarter with double-digit leads. Then something went wrong; it was almost like watching a ship sink slowly. They went from landing almost every shot to completely missing everything. They walked back into the locker room at the end of Game 2 with their heads low as they watched the championship slip between their fingers. Fans started taunting them by saying "Choke City." They were missing easy shots and seemed to let the pressure get the better of them. But all they needed was one player who would not accept defeat. Shooting guard Vernon Maxwell showed up big time and dropped 31 points in the second half of Game 3, and the team rallied for the first victory of the semifinals. They won three of the Final Four games to advance to the Conference Finals. In that series, the Utah Jazz were no match for the Rockets, who easily won the series 4–1. Houston was heading to the NBA Finals.

What made the 1994 NBA Finals so special was that you couldn't find a better matchup in NBA history. The New York Knicks were fully loaded. It was a war on the court that would last all seven games. The series was so close that every game ended within 10 points. The Rockets pulled through, won the last game of the series 90–84, and were crowned the 1994 NBA Champions. By the end of the season, fans went from cheering "Choke City" to "Clutch City," a nickname they still have today.

★ 1988-89 Detroit Pistons ★

Starting Lineup: Isiah Thomas, Joe Dumars, Adrian Dantley, Dennis Rodman, Bill Laimbeer

Season Record: 63-19

Coach: Chuck Daily

What happens when an entire basketball franchise lives up to the saying "win by any means necessary?" A team is unleashed like no other with a force that pushes until the last second of every game. Like a vicious pack of wolves, the 1988–89 Detroit Pistons devoured the competition night after night. BleacherReport.com listed the Pistons as the most hated team in NBA history. There isn't a better way to describe it: they played dirty! That's why they were nicknamed the Motor City Bad Boys.

The team was led by the trio Bill Laimbeer, Dennis Rodman, and Rick Mahom. Laimbeer was possibly the most hated player of his generation. If the NBA had superheroes, Laimbeer would have been the villain. He was notorious for flopping, or pretending to be fouled to trick the referee into blowing the whistle and calling the foul on his opponents. He is also known for getting into two major brawls with Larry Bird and Charles Barkley and for hacking

1988-89 Detroit Pistons

Joe Dumars (4) of Detroit goes up against Larry Bird of the Boston Celtics on his way to the basket. Dumars earned the honor of the 1986 Finals MVP.

23

Michael Jordan to try to limit Jordan's effectiveness. Detroit drafted Rodman in 1986 and groomed him as a player for the next three years. During their championship year, he was voted into the All-Defensive First Team. Mahom built his reputation as being extremely physical and a dirty defender long before he signed with the Pistons. If there was a player getting up from a fall, chances are Mahom had something to do with it.

Matching the defense, there were key Pistons players that gave the team an offensive edge. Guard Joe Dumars III averaged 17.6 PPG during the finals and was voted the 1986 Finals MVP. Throughout the regular season, small forward Adrian Dantley led the team in scoring with 18.4 PPG. Mark Aquirre and Vinnie Johnson came off the bench and collectively delivered 29 PPG for the season. To better understand how impressive Aquirre and Johnson were, note that they contributed more points per game than the entire bench of some NBA

Isiah Thomas (11) and Dennis Rodman are victorious after winning Game 4 and the 1989 NBA Championship against the Los Angeles Lakers.

teams. The rest of the second string were effective in their roles, which allowed the starting lineup ample time to rest and recharge. They had a full team, and everyone played with the same level of intensity.

After finishing the regular season with the best record in the NBA, the Pistons stepped up their game during the playoffs. They defensively shut down the Celtics in the first round in an easy three-game sweep. They used the exact same formula against the Milwaukee Bucks and won four straight games. They now had one goal in mind: they wanted to beat the Bulls. Detroit had a point to prove—that Chicago Bulls star Michael Jordan was not invincible. He could be stopped, and they were going to be the team to do it. Pistons coach Chuck Daily created the Jordan Rules, the defensive strategy used to limit Jordan's effectiveness.

Although they didn't stop him completely, Detroit was the most effective in slowing Jordan down compared to any team who had faced him. Ultimately, they defeated the Bulls, 4 games to 2. The Pistons advanced to the NBA Finals to face the dominant Lakers, who were undefeated during the entire playoff season up to that point. After proving themselves effective against the Bulls, the Pistons were fearless. Dumars led the assault against the Lakers and averaged 27.3 PPG. They easily won all of the Final Four games for the 1989 NBA Championship. The Bad Boys continued to be superior the following year. They won a consecutive NBA Title in 1990, which makes them one of the fiercest teams in history.

2013-14 San Antonio Spurs

Starting Lineup: Tony Parker, Danny Green, Marco Belinelli, Boris Diaw, Tim Duncan

Season Record: 62–20

Coach: Gregg Popovich

The word that best describes the next team on our countdown: family! Like small pieces of glass smoothed by the sea, the San Antonio Spurs were a consistently groomed, well-rounded team. They had a simple philosophy: play unselfish team ball. In every game, everyone passed the ball and everyone had an opportunity to shoot. Of their four NBA Championships, the season that best represents San Antonio as a unit was 2013–14. Although their individual stats per game weren't the most impressive, as a team they were extremely effective.

There have been a few trios of players in NBA history that have kept their teams at the very top of the league. From 1980–1992, the Celtics had Larry Bird, Kevin McHale, and Robert Parish. The Los Angeles Lakers of the 1980s had Magic Johnson, Kareem Abdul-Jabbar, and James Worthy. And the Chicago Bulls of the 1990s had Michael Jordan, Scottie Pippen, and Dennis Rodman.

2013-14 SAN ANTONIO SPURS

Tim Duncan (21) rises above his Miami defender to get a shot off. Duncan, along with Tony Parker and Manu Ginobili, was a core player who led his team to a winning year.

Top 10 Teams in Basketball

Somewhere at the top of this list is the most consistent trio of the twenty-first century: Tony Parker, Manu Ginobili, and Tim Duncan. Since 2003, they have carried the San Antonio Spurs to new heights. According to Fox Sports, no franchise in the NBA has a better winning percentage than the Spurs.

From 1997 until the 2015–16 season, the Spurs have consistently made the playoffs and show no signs of letting up. Fourteen of the playoffs were made with the same three core players: Parker, Ginobili, and Duncan. From the start of their career together, this trio has broken many records, including the most playoff games as an active trio in the NBA and the most wins by a trio. This last accomplishment gave the franchise the highest winning percentage in the postseason.

Tony Parker (center) and Tim Duncan (right) celebrate the 2014 NBA Championship victory with the rest of the San Antonio Spurs. They defeated the Miami Heat.

Almost everyone on the team finished the

regular season with a field goal percentage above 45 percent. Parker led the way with 16.7 PPG, 5.7 assists, and 2.2 steals. Ginobili added 12.3 PPG, 4.3 assists, and 2 steals. Duncan cleaned up nicely with 15.1 PPG, 9.7 rebounds, and 2.1 steals per game.

The Spurs had a deep roster of great offensive and defensive players. Because the team rotated during the regular games, every player received game time. Kawhi Leonard contributed 12.8 PPG and 6.2 rebounds, and Marco Belinelli averaged another 11.4 points. When including the contributions of Patrick Mills, Boris Diaw, Danny Green, Tiago Splitter, and the rest of the team, it becomes clear why the Spurs were great championship contenders.

San Antonio finished as the top seed in the regular season with a record of 62–20. The team entered the playoff season with a taste to avenge their previous season's Game 6 upset loss to the Miami Heat when Ray Allen shot a winning three-pointer. The Spurs had a full-length first round series and eventually defeated the Dallas Mavericks. The Spurs advanced past the Portland Trailblazers and the Oklahoma City Thunder in the next two rounds for the grudge match against Miami. Unlike the previous year, the Spurs were completely dominant and punished LeBron James and the Heat in a five-game series. The Spurs won the deciding four games of the 2014 NBA Finals by double digits. Now that's impressive.

2000-01 LOS ANGELES LAKERS

Starting Lineup: Ron Harper, Kobe Bryant, Rick Fox, Horace Grant, Shaquille O'Neal

Season Record: 51–31

Coach: Phil Jackson

Every team has a story, and some stories are legendary. In sports there is a line that separates great players from superstars. Franchises take chances on great players in hopes that they will be groomed into superstars. With sixteen franchise NBA Championships, the Los Angeles Lakers have a way of attracting some of the greatest players the world has ever seen. We could do a list of the top ten Lakers teams or top ten Lakers players—Wilt Chamberlain, Kareem Abdul-Jabbar, and Magic Johnson are just some of many great NBA players who have suited up in the purple, gold, and white uniforms. No matter which players they select, the results are all the same. The Lakers have a strong legacy to uphold that's rooted in pride and commitment. While there is a strong debate on which Laker team was the best, we've decided that the 2000–01 NBA Champs earned the spot on our list.

2000-01 Los Angeles Lakers

The Lakers finished the 1999–2000 season as the first-ranked team, and they won the NBA Finals. Kobe Bryant and Shaquille O'Neal formed a duo that completely dominated the league, and they averaged a combined 57 PPG throughout the regular season. Rick Fox was shooting 39 percent from the three-point range and averaging 9.6 PPG. Just before the season began, the Lakers picked up Horace Grant, who had helped Michael Jordan and the Bulls win three championships. Grant consistently pulled 7.1 rebounds and added 8.5 PPG throughout the season. He and Derrick Fisher were key defensive players until Fisher was sidelined for 62 games due to a stress fracture in his right foot. Once Fisher returned, the Lakers went on a winning streak and ended the regular season first in the Pacific Division with 56 wins.

There must have been a fuse lit inside the locker room before every postseason game because the only way to describe

Kobe Bryant (left) and Shaquille O'Neal (right) were an unstoppable duo during the 2000–01 season and led the Lakers to an NBA Championship.

Top 10 Teams in Basketball

Point guard Derek Fisher was injured during the season, but once he returned, he helped lead the team to first place in their division.

the Lakers' performance is explosive! They crushed every team they went up against and almost made it look unfair. The Blazers lost every game by double digits. The Sacramento Kings put up a better fight in the next round but proved to be inferior to the Kobe-Shaq duo. After the first two games of the 2001 Western Conference Finals, it was as if the Spurs were stripped of their confidence. San Antonio was blown out in Game 3 by 39 points and outscored again in Game 4 by 29.

League MVP and top scorer Allen Iverson led the Philadelphia 76ers to win Game 1 of the finals with 48 points to hand the Lakers their first loss of the postseason. The 76ers outshot and outrebounded LA but were no match for the onslaught of three-pointers the Lakers used to maintain the lead to win Game 2. Coach Phil Jackson directed the team to use the same formula of perimeter offense during the next three games and guided them to victory. The Lakers defended their title by going 15–1 in the postseason, which still holds the record for the best single postseason in NBA history. The following year, the Lakers defended their championship title.

2014-15 Golden State Warriors

Starting Lineup: Stephen Curry, Klay Thompson, Harrison Barnes, Draymond Green, Andrew Bogut

Season Record: 65-17

Coach: Steve Kerr

The Golden State Warriors was one of the founding franchises in the NBA and won the 1947 BAA Finals, which is considered the first NBA Championship. They were originally called the Philadelphia Warriors, but they relocated to California in 1962 and changed their name to the state's nickname, Golden State. With only four championship titles in their entire history, the last title the Warriors had won dated back to 1975. No one saw this team as a threat, but their front man Steph Curry has gained recognition as the best player in the NBA and ascended over eleven-time All-Star LeBron James.

The Warriors ended the 2013–14 regular season with a record of 51–31 and ranked sixth seed in the Western Conference. They were not a bad team, but they definitely were not playing to their full potential. After being eliminated in the first round of the playoffs, they decided to hire as head coach the one person who could

2014-15 GOLDEN STATE WARRIORS

Stephen Curry explodes into action during Game 4 of the 2015 NBA Finals. Curry is recognized as the best player in the NBA.

Top 10 Teams in Basketball

bring out their best: five-time NBA Champion Steve Kerr. Playing alongside the legendary Michael Jordan with the Chicago Bulls, Kerr knew what it took to make a championship team. By the end of the next season, he had already broken the record for the most wins by a rookie coach, and he was the first rookie coach to win a championship since Pat Riley in 1982.

The team was already intact and came into the 2014–15 season with only a few minor adjustments to its second string. They added Harrison Barnes and Draymond Green to their starting lineup. Andrew Bogut protected the rim as their center. Because the team didn't miss many shots, his job was made a lot easier. Bogut averaged 6.3 PPG with 8.1 total rebounds. In the previous season, Klay Thompson and Steph Curry were nicknamed the Splash Brothers for setting the

Klay Thompson, the other half of Golden State's Splash Brothers, shoots against J. R. Smith of the Cleveland Cavaliers during Game 6 of the 2015 NBA Finals.

record for the most three-pointers made by a pair of teammates in a single season (484). By the end of 2015, the pair broke its record by sinking 525 shots from beyond the arch. Draymond Green was also an important fixture in the lineup with an average of 11.7 points and 8.2 total rebounds per game. Harrison Barnes contributed 10.1 points and 5.5 rebounds per game.

If the regular season was a test, the Warriors aced it with flying colors. They finished with the league's best record at 67–15. All the critics said the Warriors had one of the easiest postseason journeys to the NBA Finals. They swept the eighth-placed New Orleans Pelicans in a four-game series. The Memphis Grizzlies put up more of a fight and won two of their six-game series, and the Houston Rockets were eliminated after five games. LeBron James led the Cleveland Cavilers to two victories in the finals, but his efforts were not enough for the Splash Brothers' assault. The Warriors became the 2015 NBA Champions.

The trick was in coach Kerr's decision to run with a small-ball team lineup. In basketball, *small ball* describes a squad that sacrifices height for physical strength and speed. The Warriors' small ball concept worked because they had the best shooters and fast players on the court—full of energy—while the defending star players on Cleveland were already fatigued from playing most of the game. Golden State was also extremely focused, as their second string often played like they were starting players. It's hard to know who to guard when everyone has the ability to score. In the opening of the 2015–16 season, they were out to prove that their title was not a fluke.

2012-13 Miami Heat

Starting Lineup: Mario Chalmers, Dwyane Wade, Shane Battier, LeBron James, Chris Bosh

Season Record: 62–20

Coach: Erik Spoelstra

When we take a look at today's athletes at the top of their games, a man very worthy of his nickname, King James, sits near the top of the list. Four-time NBA MVP, LeBron James remains a force on the court. James is at the top of almost every NBA record. As of early 2016, he had taken his teams to six of the last nine NBA Finals. Along with the rest of the Miami Heat, he has snatched two championship rings—in 2012 and 2013.

Entering the 2012–13 NBA season, there was no team hotter than the Miami Heat. They were the defending champions and topped the Oklahoma Thunder by 4 games to 1 in the 2011–12 NBA Finals. The core of Miami's team featured their Big Three: Dwyane Wade, who averaged 21.2 points, 5.1 assists, and 5 rebounds; Chris Bosh, who snagged an additional 16.6 points and 6.8 rebounds; and LeBron James, who ruled with 26.8 points and 8 rebounds per game.

2012-13 MIAMI HEAT

San Antonio's Manu Ginobili faces some tough defense as he tries to shoot against Chris Bosh (1) and Ray Allen (34) of the Miami Heat.

Top 10 Teams in Basketball

LeBron James (left) holds his NBA Finals MVP award while Dwyane Wade (right) cradles the team's Championship Trophy after winning Game 7 against the San Antonio Spurs.

2012-13 MIAMI HEAT

If this trio wasn't scary enough, the Heat added Mario Chalmers, Chane Battier, and Ray Allen. What made this team so dynamic was the many weapons it had in almost every player on its roster. They had an amazing regular season run and led the league with a 66–16 record. Over the course of the season, Miami went on a 27-game winning streak, the second longest in NBA history.

The Heat entered the NBA Playoffs with all the fuel from their outstanding regular season performance. They dismembered the Milwaukee Bucks within four games and won every game in the first round by double digits. The Chicago Bulls snatched the first game of the second round, but Miami bounced back to defeat them in a five-game series. In the Eastern Conference Finals, the Indiana Pacers were not going to give up without a fight, and they tied the series in Game 6 but ultimately caved to the Heat with a 23-point blowout loss in the final game.

Leading up to the 2013 finals, the San Antonio Spurs' head coach Gregg Popovich must have studied the Eastern Conference Finals because the Spurs let out a team assault that snatched a victory in Game 1. In Game 2, Mario Chalmers scored 19 points, which helped Miami win. The next few games were like a tennis match; both teams were not backing down. But something magical happens when LeBron's back is against the wall—he performs at another level. During the final game, he put up 37 points, 12 rebounds, 4 assists, and 2 steals. The Heat closed the casket on a long, well-earned postseason as defending champs. Miami continued to thrive during following season and became the second team since the 1998 Chicago Bulls to win a three-peat in the Eastern Conference and the 2014 NBA Finals.

1995-96 Chicago Bulls

Starting Lineup: Steve Kerr, Michael Jordan, Scottie Pippen, Dennis Rodman, Luc Loongley

Season Record: 70–12

Coach: Phil Jackson

There's no doubt about it, the 1995–96 Chicago Bulls are the hottest team in the history of the NBA. This team was led by three of the best defenders of all time: Scottie Pippen, Dennis Rodman, and, of course, Michael Jordan. However, if you think their game stopped at defense, think again! The Chicago Bulls had it all: a fully-loaded bench and a league-leading offensive lineup. They proved this by ending the season with the best record in NBA history: 72–10. No team had ever won more than 70 games during the regular season.

From 1990–93, Jordan led the Bulls to three consecutive championships before retiring to play professional baseball. He announced his return to hoops in 1995. In the 1995 NBA Playoffs, the Orlando Magic faced the Bulls and proved to be the team in better shape. They stopped Chicago 4 games to 2 in the second

1995-96 CHICAGO BULLS

Scottie Pippen (left) of the Chicago Bulls drives past Detlef Schrempf of the Seattle SuperSonics as Michael Jordan (right) clears out the lane during Game 6 of the NBA Finals.

Top 10 Teams in Basketball

Michael "Air" Jordan makes a leaping pass look easy during the NBA Finals against Seattle.

1995-96 CHICAGO BULLS

round of the playoffs. Chicago made two major trades to add Dennis Rodman and Jack Haley to their roster. During the 1995–96 season, the Bulls proved to be far superior to every opponent they faced. It was difficult to know which players to guard because every man on the team put up points.

Jordan was the top scorer with an average of 30.4 PPG. Pippen led the per-game assist total with 5.9, and Rodman had a team high of 14.9 rebounds per game. When the star players needed help, the rest of the team proved why they were champions. Including their bench, every player on the Bulls' roster put up points and rebounds per game. Toni Kukoc came off Chicago's bench and made NBA Sixth Man of the Year, Steve Kerr held the season's second in three-point field goal percentage, Luc Longley averaged 9.1 PPG, and Ron Harper put up 7.4 PPG.

The Bulls owned a certain level of finesse and made every game look like practice. During the Bulls' championship dynasty, they never lost more than two games in a row. It was a group of guys that you hated to see play against your favorite team but you loved to watch execute with such precision and accuracy. You couldn't find players who wanted to win more than they did. The team's passion is what put them on top. They won the championship against the Seattle SuperSonics in a 4–2 game series. The Bulls remained the dominant force in basketball for the next two years. They won the next two championships for their first three-peat. Two years later, Michael Jordan returned to lead the Bulls to their second three-peat for a total of six NBA Championships in eight years. The legendary Chicago Bulls remain the best team in NBA history.

Glossary

BAA Finals—The first official NBA Finals competition.

Basketball Association of America (BAA)—A professional men's basketball league in America that ran from 1946–49.

Big Three—A term given to the three most dominating players on a basketball team.

clutch—In sports, a term used to describe a critical situation in which the outcome of the game is at stake.

Eastern Conference Finals—One of two conference final tournaments in the NBA; each conference is made of fifteen teams and organized into three divisions.

field goal percentage—The ratio of goals made verses the goals attempted within a basketball game.

flopping—An intentional fall by a player to falsely draw a personal foul against an opponent.

Jordan Rules—A defensive strategy created by Isiah Thomas in 1988 that was used by the Detroit Pistons to limit Michael Jordan's effectiveness on offense.

Midwest Division—One of three divisions in the Western Conference of the NBA.

National Basketball League (NBL)—One of two major professional men's basketball leagues in America; established in 1937.

NBA franchise—An entire team and staff of an NBA team.

NBA Playoffs—The best-of-seven-games elimination tournament for the top sixteen teams in the NBA; the top eight teams are selected from each conference.

second string—Players who are used to replace or relieve those who start a game.

starting lineup—The five players per team who will actively participate at the start of the basketball game.

stress fracture—A small crack or severe bruising within a bone caused by overuse and repetitive activity.

three-peat—A term used to describe winning three consecutive championships.

24-second shot clock—A countdown clock to show the amount of time the offensive team can possess the basketball before shooting, which quickens the pace of the game.

Western Conference Finals—One of two conference final tournaments in the NBA; each conference is made of fifteen teams and organized by three divisions.

Further Reading

Books

Buckley Jr, James. *Chicago Bulls on the Hardwood.* Minneapolis, MN: Lerner Publishing, 2013.

Graves, Will. *The Best NBA Teams of All Time.* Edina, MN: ABDO Publishing Company, 2013.

Kelley, K.C. *Basketball Superstars 2016.* New York: Scholastic, 2015.

Silverman, Drew. *NBA Finals.* Edina, MN: ABDO Publishing Company, 2013.

Websites

Basketball Reference
basketball-reference.com
Includes statistics on every player in NBA history.

Jr. NBA
jr.nba.com
Sections include "Skills and Drills," "About the Game," and "Fun Zone."

National Basketball Association
nba.com
Loaded with everything NBA: player profiles, scores, stats, standings, news, and highlight videos, as well as "Kids Club Fun and Games."

Index

A
Abdul-Jabbar, Kareem, 5, 26, 30
Allen, Ray, 14, 29, 41

B
BAA Finals, 34
Basketball Association of America (BAA), 4, 34
Big Three, 14–17, 38
Bryant, Kobe, 16–17, 31
Bulls, 11, 25–26, 31, 36, 41–45

C
Celtics, 4, 14–17, 25–26
clutch, 13, 21
Curry, Stephen, 34, 36

D
Duncan, Tim, 28–29

E
Eastern Conference, 4, 15–16, 41

F
field goal percentage, 29, 45
flopping, 22
franchise, 4, 6, 14, 17, 22, 28, 30, 34

G
Garnett, Kevin, 14–15

H
Hall of Fame, 6
Heat, 13, 29, 38–41

I
Iverson, Allen, 6, 9, 33

J
James, LeBron, 13, 29, 34, 37–38, 41
Johnson, Magic, 5, 26, 30
Jordan, Michael, 24–26, 31, 36, 42, 45
Jordan Rules, 25

L
Lakers, 4, 13, 16–17, 25–26, 30–33

M
Mavericks, 10–13, 29
Midwest Division, 21
Most Valuable Player (MVP) Award, 18, 24, 33, 38
Motor City Bad Boys, 22

N
National Basketball League (NBL), 4
NBA Draft, 10
Nowitzki, Dirk, 10–13

O
Olajuwon, Hakeem, 18, 20–21
O'Neal, Shaquille, 31, 33

P
Pippen, Scottie, 26, 42, 45
Pistons, 16, 22–25

R
Rockets, 18–21, 37
Rodman, Dennis, 22, 24, 26, 42, 45

S
second string, 25, 36–37
76ers, 6–9, 33
small ball, 37
Splash Brothers, 36–37
Spurs, 26–29, 33, 41
starting lineup, 6, 25, 36

T
three-peat, 41, 45
24-second shot clock, 4

W
Wade, Dwayne, 13, 38
Warriors, 4, 18, 34–37
Western Conference, 4, 11, 21, 33–34